PONTARDDULAIS
SW. 882822
16/18

2 0 NOV

D0865694

m—S

go to School

Roger Hargreaves

Hello, my name is Walter. Can you spot me in this book?

Original concept by
Roger Hargreaves

Written and illustrated by
Adam Hargreaves

LLYFRGELLOEDD ABERTAWE
SWANSEA LIBRARIES

WITHDRAWN

8500003237

Little Miss Tiny was very excited.

It was her first day at school.

She was so excited she woke up extra early.

And she got to school so early that it was not even open when she arrived.

The only other person there was Little Miss Late.

But she was not early.

She was late.

A whole term late!

When everyone else got there, they had to hang their bags on their pegs.

Mr Muddle's bag was so heavy that it bent his peg.

And why was it so heavy?

Mr Muddle had brought a sack full of rocks to school.

A rock-sack rather than a rucksack!

What a muddly old muddle he is.

Little Miss Tiny was looking forward to learning lots of new things at school.

Her teacher was Little Miss Sunshine.

Little Miss Tiny gave her an apple.

But before Little Miss Sunshine could say 'thank you' Mr Greedy had gobbled it up.

In one bite!

CRUNCH!

Little Miss Tiny had learnt her first lesson of the day.

Don't leave food within Mr Greedy's reach!

The first proper lesson of the day was writing.

Little Miss Tiny very carefully copied the letters Little Miss Sunshine had written on the board.

Unlike Mr Messy!

And then it was story time.

Read by Little Miss Chatterbox.

Who knew how to make a short story long.

Very,
very,
very long!

Little Miss Tiny was rather glad to escape out into the playground at break time.

She had a great time on the slide and in the sandpit and she made a friend.

Mr Small.

He was almost the same size as Mr Greedy's snack!

And then it was painting time.

Little Miss Sunshine asked them to paint their favourite thing.

Little Miss Tiny painted a daisy.

Little Miss Dotty painted lots of dots.

Mr Topsy-Turvy painted his cat.

And Mr Greedy painted …

… a sausage!

Little Miss Tiny was very happy at lunchtime.

She got to sit next to Mr Small.

They had a tiny portion and a small portion to eat.

Half a sausage and five peas each.

After lunch it was show and tell.

Little Miss Naughty had brought her rubber spider.

Little Miss Bossy, the headmistress, was not happy.

Not at all happy!

Little Miss Tiny was very happy when they went on to maths.

Little Miss Sunshine had written a sum on the board.

"What is two plus two?" she asked.

Little Miss Tiny was about to answer 'four', but someone answered before her.

"Two plus two equals five hundred and seventy three point one and two halves," cried Mr Wrong.

Oh dear, when Mr Wrong gets something wrong, he gets it really, really wrong!

And then it was time for games.

Mr Silly was their PE teacher.

Nobody could work out what sport they were supposed to be playing!

But it was great fun.

Little Miss Tiny was rather sad when the bell rang for the end of school.

And that night as she lay in bed she remembered all the fun things she had done that day.